A Berry Lucky St. Patrick's Day

By Mickie Matheis
Illustrated by Laura Thomas

Grosset & Dunlap
An Imprint of Penguin Group (USA) LLC

GROSSET & DUNLAP
Published by the Penguin Group
Penguin Group (USA) LLC, 375 Hudson Street, New York, New York 10014, USA

USA | Canada | UK | Ireland | Australia | New Zealand | India | South Africa | China

penguin.com
A Penguin Random House Company

ISBN 978-0-448-48420-4   10 9 8 7 6 5 4 3 2 1

Berry Bitty City was a sea of green!

It was St. Patrick's Day, and the residents of the tiny town were busy getting ready for the annual parade and festival to be held that afternoon.

4

Strawberry Shortcake was hard at work in her café. She had created a new smoothie flavor especially for the occasion.

"I'm calling it the Magical Mint Smoothie," she explained to Pupcake and Custard as she slowly poured the foamy green liquid into pitchers. "I hope everyone likes it."

Her friends were busy with their own chores, too.

Raspberry Torte had just finished sewing costumes for a troupe of Berrykin dancers who were performing in the parade. She had chosen an orange-and-green patchwork design with matching green caps.

"The Berrykins are going to look berry adorable in these," Raspberry thought.

Meanwhile, Plum Pudding and Cherry Jam were rehearsing with the dancers at Sweet Beats Studio. Cherry played a lively tune on her keyboard while the Berrykins jumped and spun to the music.

"Great job!" Plum said, clapping enthusiastically as the Berrykins ended the routine with their big finish—a pyramid. "You're going to be a hit!"

Across town at the Orange Mart, Orange Blossom was hiding chocolate coins wrapped in gold foil for a scavenger hunt.

"What a fruitastically fun idea!" Blueberry Muffin remarked.

"Thank you!" replied Orange, carefully placing some coins on a shelf lined with boxes. "I thought this would be a cute holiday game since leprechauns collect gold coins."

"I hope everyone likes my St. Patrick's Day crafts," Blueberry said. She stood at a table surrounded by supplies.

"Oh, I'm sure they will," said Orange. "You're berry creative."

The girls agreed that the St. Patrick's Day festivities were shaping up to be the best ever!

Everyone was happy and excited . . .

. . . except for poor Lemon Meringue.
Lemon was not having any luck getting ready for the holiday!

First, the lime squares she baked burned in the oven.

Then the special hair dye she mixed together came out wrong. She had wanted to color her hair green for the day, but it turned brown instead.

Finally, the headpieces she was making to go with Raspberry's costumes weren't coming out correctly. They didn't look anything like the picture in the book Lemon had gotten from Blueberry's bookstore.

When Strawberry came to Lemon's salon to pick up the headpieces for Raspberry,
she found her friend petting her dog, Henna, and looking sad.
"What's wrong?" Strawberry asked with concern.

"I'm having the worst luck today," Lemon replied.
"I can't seem to do anything right." She went on to tell
Strawberry how badly her day was going.

Strawberry patted Lemon's hand. "I'm sure things will get better,"
she said kindly. She told her friend she had to run some other errands but
offered to return later to help her.

Strawberry left the salon and immediately went to the Orange Mart. She called the other girls together and told them how terrible Lemon's day had been. Then she told everyone her plan for helping Lemon believe in herself again.

"Let's plant a four-leaf clover for Lemon to find," Strawberry suggested. "Then she'll think her luck has returned."

The girls searched through the grass around Orange's store for more than an hour, but they couldn't find a single four-leaf clover! How would they ever help Lemon feel better?

Suddenly Strawberry smiled. "Don't worry, girls. I have an idea!" she said.

When she finished explaining her plan, the other girls nodded eagerly. It just might work!

Raspberry found a clover with three large leaves, and Cherry plucked an extra leaf from another clover.

Using Blueberry's glue gun, they attached the extra leaf to the three-leaf clover. Amazing! It looked just like a four-leaf clover!

"It's perfect—thanks, girls!" Strawberry said happily.

Strawberry hurried back to Lemon's salon with Pupcake and Custard.
She planted the clover right by the edge of the step leading up to Lemon's front porch.

"Stay here," she whispered to her pets. "When Lemon comes outside, make sure she sees the clover."

A short time later, Lemon came out of her salon with Henna. She watched as her dog bounded over to Pupcake and Custard. That's when she spotted the clover in the grass. "Could it be?" she wondered. She carefully lifted her discovery from the ground.

"Wow—just what I need!" she exclaimed. "If this doesn't bring me good luck, nothing will!"

Lemon ran back inside and got to work.

Over the next hour, Lemon baked several batches of lime squares, and they were all delicious. She mixed a new bottle of hair dye and tinted her hair a lovely shade of green. And this time when she tried making headpieces for the Berrykin dancers, they turned out just right.

Later at the festival, Lemon told her friends about the four-leaf clover.
"I was lucky to find it," she said. "Otherwise, everything would still be going wrong."
The girls looked at one another and smiled.

Strawberry put her arm around Lemon and told her friend what they had done. "We wanted you to feel better, but you really didn't need luck," Strawberry assured her. "You just needed a little reminder of how amazing you truly are."

Lemon looked around at her friends. "Well, I guess I never lost my luck after all," she said thoughtfully.

"Why do you say that?" Strawberry asked.

Lemon put her arms around the girls and gave them a squeeze. "Because I have all of you as my berry best friends—and that makes me the luckiest girl in the world!"